For Mum, Dad and Nick – J.K.
For the amazing Isabella – D.W.

Text copyright © 2004 by Joanna Kenrick. Illustrations copyright © 2004 by Doffy Weir.
The rights of Joanna Kenrick and Doffy Weir to be identified as the author and illustrator of this work
have been asserted by them in accordance with the Copyright, Designs and Patents Act, 1988.

First published in Great Britain in 2004 by Andersen Press Ltd., 20 Vauxhall Bridge Road, London SW1V 2SA.
Published in Australia by Random House Australia Pty., 20 Alfred Street, Milsons Point, Sydney, NSW 2061.
All rights reserved. Colour separated in Switzerland by Photolitho AG, Zürich.
Printed and bound in Singapore by Tien Wah Press.

10   9   8   7   6   5   4   3   2   1

British Library Cataloguing in Publication Data available.

ISBN 1 84270 324 2

This book has been printed on acid-free paper

Moondance

story by Joanna Kenrick

and pictures by Doffy Weir

Andersen Press
London

"Tell me again," begged Teeho.
His big sister Terin took a deep breath.
"Every year," she said mysteriously,
"when the moon is in the eucalyptus trees,
all the tigers in the country come together
for the Moondance."
"And what is the Moondance?" breathed Teeho.
He knew the answer but it was
still exciting to hear it.
"All the tigers make a giant circle.
Each tiger takes hold of the tail in front of him.
Then they dance in the light of the eucalyptus moon,"
said Terin.

"And why do they dance?" asked Teeho.

"The dance shows that all tigers, no matter where they live, are all part of one family," said Terin.

"And when will the moon be in the eucalyptus trees?" asked Teeho.

"In three days' time," said Terin.

Teeho bounced up and down. "I can't wait! It will be so exciting to dance with my family in the moonlight!"

"Oh no," said Terin, shaking her head.
"You can't dance. You're too little."
"Too little?" cried Teeho.
"You can't join the Moondance
until you are six months old,"
said Terin.
She flicked a fly off her ear.
"That's the rule."
"That's not fair!" cried Teeho.
"It's no good sulking," said Terin.
But Teeho couldn't help it.

"Mummy," he asked, "why can't I join the Moondance?"
His mummy nuzzled his ear. "Because you're too little," she said.
"No, I'm not," grumbled Teeho.
"I'm sorry, Teeho," said his mummy. "It's the rule."

"Daddy," said Teeho,
"why can't I join the Moondance?"
His daddy twitched his tail.
"Because only grown-up tigers can
join the Moondance," he said.
"I am grown up!" protested Teeho.
"I'm sorry, Teeho," said his daddy.
"It's the rule."
"I hate rules," said Teeho,
and off he stomped.

Teeho stomped for quite a while
but it didn't make him feel any better.
He just felt hot and bothered.
So he went to the water hole to have a drink.

"Hello, Teeho!" called his friend Quark from the trees.
"You look sad."

"No one will let me join in the Moondance,"
said Teeho crossly. "It's the rule."
"Oh dear," said Quark.
He thought for a moment. "Is there a rule
that says you can't do your own Moondance?"
"No," said Teeho. "But it wouldn't be any fun
to dance on my own."

"Why not?" asked Quark.
"I often fly on my own. I can choose
where I fly to and how high and how fast.
If you dance on your own you can
choose your own steps.

You don't have to do what everyone else does."

"What a good idea," said Teeho.
"I can make my own Moondance.
Then everyone will see how good
I am and maybe they'll let me
join in! Thank you, Quark!"

And he bounded off to find a place to start practising.

For the next three days
Teeho practised his dance.

He practised in the heat of the day . . .

He practised in the dark of night.

"Where have you been?"
his mummy asked.

"IT'S a secret," replied Teeho.

"Where have you been?"
his daddy asked.

"It's a SECRET," replied Teeho.

"Where have you been?"
his big sister Terin asked.

"IT'S A SECRET!" replied Teeho.

He couldn't tell anyone. Not yet.

At last came the night when the moon
was in the eucalyptus trees.
Tigers began to arrive from all over the country:
old tigers, young tigers, big tigers, little tigers.

But not one of them was as little as Teeho.
He began to feel a bit nervous.
"What if nobody likes my dance?"
he wondered.

But the time had come
for the Moondance to begin.
All the tigers stood in a circle
and took hold of the tail
in front of them.

There was complete silence.
The tigers began to dance,
slowly at first, and then faster and faster.
Soon they were a whirling mass
of orange and black stripes.

And just as the dance was at its most frantic,
Teeho stepped out into the moonlight.
Paws shaking with nerves, he started to perform
his own Moondance:

One step forward, one step back.
A twist to the side and a twirl of the tail.

   One step forward,
   one step back.
   A twist to the side
   and a twirl of the tail.

The circle of tigers slowed down.
"Look!" whispered Terin, her mouth full of tail.
"It's Teeho! What's he doing?"
"It looks like he's doing his own Moondance," said an old tiger.
A hush fell over the circle as they all turned to watch
the little tiger leaping, bounding and twirling:

One step forward, one step back.
A twist to the side and a twirl of the tail.

One step forward,
one step back.
A twist to the side
and a twirl of the tail.

"It's wonderful,"
said a tiger from the East.

"I want to try it,"
said a tiger from the West.

"How does it go?"
asked a tiger from the North.

"One step forward, one step back.
A twist to the side and a twirl of the tail,"
said a tiger from the South.

Soon, everyone was trying
Teeho's Moondance:

One step forward, one step back.
A twist to the side and a twirl of the tail.
One step forward, one step back.
A twist to the side and a twirl of the tail.

"Look, Teeho!" called Quark.
"They're doing your dance!"

Teeho looked up.
He had been so wrapped up
in his own dance, he hadn't noticed
what was going on around him.
Everywhere he looked, tigers were dancing —
his dance, the one he had made up himself.
Nobody was telling him he was too little.
Everyone was having fun.

Teeho felt so happy
he thought he would burst.
"I told you!" he called to Quark.
"I told you I would join in!
I *can* do the Moondance!"

And he went to join the crowd
in his very own dance
under the eucalyptus moon . . .